AUGUSTUS AND HIS
SMILE

CATHERINE RAYNER

LITTLE TIGER PRESS
London

Augustus the tiger was sad.

He had lost his smile.

So he did a HUGE tigery stretch

and set off to find it.

First he crept
under a cluster
of bushes. He found
a small, shiny beetle,
but he couldn't see
his smile.

Then he climbed to the tops of the tallest trees.
He found birds that chirped and called,
but he couldn't find his smile.

Further and further Augustus searched.

He scaled the crests of the highest mountains where the snow clouds swirled, making frost patterns in the freezing air.

He swam to the bottom of the deepest oceans
and splished and splashed with shoals of tiny, shiny fish.

He pranced and paraded through the
largest desert, making shadow shapes
in the sun. Augustus padded further

and further

through shifting sand

until . . .

... pitter

    patter

        pitter

          patter

             drip

                drop

                    plop!

Augustus danced and raced as raindrops bounced and flew.

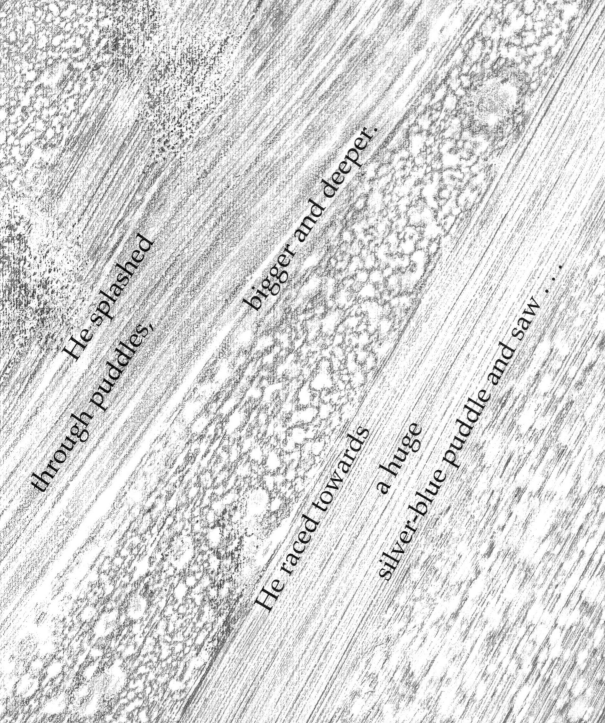

He splashed
through puddles,

bigger and deeper.

He raced towards
a huge
silver-blue puddle and saw . . . .

. . . there, under his nose

. . . his smile!

And Augustus realised that his smile would be there,
whenever he was happy.

He only had to swim with the fish
or dance in the puddles,
or climb the mountains and look at the world –
for happiness was everywhere around him.

Augustus was so pleased that
he hopped

and skipped . . .

. . . and jumped away,

smiling.